Glamour! * Talent!

Stardom!

Fame and fortune
uld be one step away!

Welcome to *

Fame
School

D0550591

A 80   01 540241

For another fix of

read

Reach for the Stars
Rising Star
Secret Ambition
Rivals!
Tara's Triumph
Lucky Break
Solo Star
Christmas Stars
Pop Diva
Battle of the Bands
Star Maker
Dancing Star
Summer Spectacular

Fame School

Trick or Treat

Cindy Jefferies

USBORNE

For David, Brooke and Colby, with love

First published in 2010 by Usborne Publishing Ltd., Usborne House,
83-85 Saffron Hill, London EC1N 8RT, England. www.usborne.com

A CIP catalogue record for this book is available from the British Library.

JFMAM JASOND/10 00534/1

ISBN 9781409509769

Printed in Reading, Berkshire, UK.

1 Just Not Funny

Danny James was one of the best drummers at Rockley Park, the fantastic school that taught talented students how to make it in the music business. At lunchtimes, Danny could usually be found with his friends, discussing the morning's lessons, but today he was sitting on his own, ignoring his sandwich and staring into space.

"Hi there!" said Pop Lowther, as she and her twin sister, Lolly, passed him on their way to collect some lunch. He didn't reply. In fact he didn't even seem to have *seen* them.

"What's up with him?" said Pop as they lined up with the rest of their friends to choose their food.

Lolly shrugged. "Perhaps he didn't hear us. It is quite noisy in here."

"Here comes Marmalade," said Pop. "I bet Danny notices *him*."

"Well, you can't really ignore Marmalade, can you?" Lolly smiled. "He doesn't let you."

They watched, as the ginger-haired dancer wove his way gracefully between the tables towards them. Marmalade paused at Danny's table and said something. Then he ruffled his friend's hair, but Danny shook him off, grumpily.

"Guess what?" Marmalade bounced up to Pop and Lolly a few seconds later, grabbed a tray and joined the queue. "I've made a Halloween resolution."

"Isn't New Year the time for resolutions?" said Chloe, who was further along in the queue.

Marmalade nodded. "But that doesn't mean you can't make them at other times as well."

"So what is this great resolution then?" asked Chloe.

"Well, you know how it's Halloween on Sunday?"

"*Yes,*" everyone chorused. It was impossible to ignore with the TV, magazines and shops full of Halloween merchandise.

"Well I've decided to try to play a trick on each person in our year by the end of Halloween. That gives me four-and-a-half days from now. Do you reckon I'll manage it?"

"Oh no," groaned Ed, who shared a room with Marmalade, Danny and their other friend, Ben. "Can you get mine over and done with first? I don't want to spend the next few days wondering if a spider is going to appear in my bed."

"You mean one like this?" Marmalade pulled a handful of bits and pieces out of his pocket and extracted a large hairy spider, which he dangled in front of Ed.

"Where did you get all this stuff?" Chloe giggled. She bent down and retrieved a bloodstained fingertip and a couple of plastic flies that had spilled from his hand. "And if you're planning on tricking *us*, I hope you're going to do the same to the school ghost that's supposed to haunt the corridors at this time of year."

"Oh not *that* old story," sighed Tara. She put her hand on her heart and spoke in a deep TV presenter voice. "*Poor daughter of Rockley Park House, who fell to her death from the rooftop walk, while rehearsing for a concert for her parents in Victorian times.*" She grinned at Chloe. "You'll have all the year seven girls squealing in terror again like last year. Don't anyone dare spread gossip about it; we don't want them waking us up with their nightmares!"

Chloe laughed, but Pop didn't look so amused. "She *might* be real," she insisted. "And isn't she supposed to appear when something dreadful is about to happen? I'd *die* if I ever saw her!"

"Thanks, Chloe." Marmalade took the collection of horrible items from her. "I don't think I'll bother with the ghost," he said with a grin. "It would be a bit difficult playing a trick on something I don't believe in it."

He stuffed the plastic tricks back into his pocket. "I brought this lot from home at the beginning of term," he said. "I thought they might come in useful."

Lolly laughed. "Only you would consider plastic flies and," she shuddered extravagantly, "hairy spiders *useful*."

"Well, you'd better get a move on if you're going to trick us all before bedtime on Sunday," said Tara. "It's Wednesday already. Or are you hoping some people will buy you off with treats instead?"

"Nah," said Marmalade. "You're all going to be tricked, whatever you offer me. But you're right. I ought to get going." He looked at all his friends in turn and smiled slowly. "Hmm," he pondered, stroking his chin. "Now who's going to be my first victim?"

"No point in making it any of us at the moment," said Ben with a laugh. "We're all ready for you and your pocketful of horrors."

"How about Danny?" said Pop. "He hasn't seen them, has he?"

"Not recently," said Marmalade. "Excellent suggestion, Pop. Thanks. I may try not to terrify you too much when it comes to your turn."

Pop glared at Marmalade and he laughed.

Trick or Treat

Marmalade left the queue and made his way back to Danny. His friend still had a half-eaten sandwich in front of him, and his drink hadn't been touched. Marmalade sat down, looked towards the door and said, "Whatever is Charlie doing bringing a cymbal into the dining room?"

Danny followed his gaze and, quick as a flash, Marmalade pushed the plastic fingertip into the sandwich.

"You idiot!" said Danny. "It's a folder, not a cymbal."

"Silly me," said Marmalade, glancing at Danny's sandwich. The finger was sticking out, with the bloodstained nail in full view. He waited for Danny to notice it, but he didn't. Instead, he picked up the sandwich and took an absent-minded bite. Marmalade held his breath. Then, as Danny chewed, he wondered if he ought to say something. He didn't want his friend to choke. But, before he could speak, Danny put the sandwich down and peered at it.

"There's something in here," he said, crossly. "The kitchen staff should be more careful. I might have…"

He pulled the butter-smeared fingertip out and stared at it. "How did *that* get there?"

Marmalade exploded with laughter and slapped the table with his hand in delight. "You should see your *face*! For a second there I was afraid you were going to swallow the whole thing. Don't you *ever* look at what you're eating?"

Danny glared at Marmalade. "Why don't you just grow up?" he snapped.

Marmalade grinned. "You know me," he said easily. "Anything for a laugh. And you must admit, it was funny." He grinned at Danny, sure that he would see the funny side once he'd thought about it. But Danny didn't look even slightly amused. He shoved his plate away angrily, and Marmalade only just managed to stop it from flying off the table. "Hey! Don't be like that."

Danny got up and glared at his friend. "Get lost, will you? I'm not in the mood. Just because you think life is one long laugh it doesn't mean it is." He pushed past Marmalade and headed out of the door.

Trick or Treat

"That went well!" said Ed, cheerfully, plonking his tray of food on the table.

"What's up with him?" said Ben, taking a seat.

"I don't know," said Marmalade. "He's been a bit moody these last few days, but he's never been quite like this before. I thought the trick would make him laugh, once he'd recovered from the shock."

"Is Danny okay?" said Chloe, arriving with the rest of the girls.

"No," said Marmalade. "I don't know what's wrong, but I don't think he's okay at all."

2 A Friend Who Cares

It was very unlike Danny to be so moody. Although he was quiet, usually he was easy-going and happy. He was a very popular student so everyone wanted to help cheer him up, but no one knew what was wrong.

"He might talk to you, Chloe," said Lolly. "You two have been good friends for such a long time."

"Or Marmalade," said Chloe, looking at him. "The two of you are really good friends as well."

Marmalade looked dejectedly at the abandoned sandwich. "Well I thought so," he said, picking up the plastic finger. "But maybe we're not."

"Well there's no point us all asking him," said Tara.

"Or he'll get even more fed up."

"But we can't do anything to help until we know what's upsetting him," said Pop. "Chloe, why don't you talk to him this afternoon after lessons? I'm sure he'll open up to you."

"And just talking about it will help, I'm sure," said Lolly. "It always does for me."

Chloe did her best to catch Danny after French, which was the last lesson of the day, but he darted out of the classroom before she could get to him. She hung around for a while in case he'd gone to the loo, and looked in the library, but there was no sign of him. "I can't find him anywhere," she told Marmalade, who was about to head back to his room. "I wonder if he's gone to do some drum practice."

"Maybe," said Marmalade. "Never mind. He's sure to turn up for tea, and if you don't manage to get him alone after that I'll see him in our room later."

"Okay." Chloe looked at Marmalade. "You're not going to let this stop you in your quest to trick us all by Halloween, are you?"

Marmalade looked uncomfortable. "Well I don't know…it seems…"

Chloe took his arm and squeezed it. "Come on, Marmalade. We're not going to cheer Danny up if we *all* start going round with long faces. Life wouldn't be the same if you stopped messing about. We *rely* on you."

"Well…all right." He gave Chloe a hug and a big grin. "I'd better get going then, if I'm going to reach my target. Thanks!" He sped off, leaving an unsuspecting Chloe with a large hairy spider attached to the back of her jacket.

Chloe missed Danny again at tea.

"He was only here for about ten minutes, to scoff his food," said Charlie, who was the other drummer in their year. "He told me he was going to spend the evening practising. Has he got a gig on TV or something? He's gone into practice overdrive."

"I don't think so," Chloe replied. "But I don't know." Charlie and Danny weren't especially close friends, so Chloe didn't want to gossip. She turned to go and Charlie let out a loud laugh.

"What?" Chloe gave him a confused look.

Charlie shook his head. "Nothing," he said, and hurried away.

Chloe went to join the rest of her friends, who were gathering at their usual table in the dining room. She hung her bag over a chair and turned to go back for her tea.

Pop let out a loud scream. "Chloe…CHLOE!"

"Get it off! Get it OFF!" added Lolly, flapping at Chloe's back with a napkin.

"What is it?" asked Chloe, trying to stay calm in the face of the twins' panic. Surely whatever it was couldn't hurt her? It wasn't the season for wasps.

"Calm down, girls," said Ben, getting up and coming round to their side of the table. "I'll get it. Just stand still a moment… Ah."

Pop and Lolly were huddled together, hardly daring to look as Ben bravely removed the offending article from Chloe's jacket with his bare hand. "Do you want this, Chloe? Or shall I shove it down Marmalade's neck?"

The plastic spider lay in his hand. Chloe laughed. She didn't have a problem with spiders, but Pop and Lolly hated them. She took it from Ben and tossed it over to Marmalade with a grin. "Well done!" she said. "I think that counts as tricking four of us in one go, don't you?"

Marmalade gave her a wink.

After supper, Marmalade went straight back to the boarding house, to see if he could find Danny. Ed and Ben had gone to jam with some others in the Rock Department, and so Marmalade hoped he'd have a chance to speak to Danny on his own. He met his friend at the door, clutching his drumsticks. He was on his way out.

"Hi!"

"Hi." Danny still sounded more subdued than usual.

"What's up, mate?" asked Marmalade, falling into step with his friend as he headed back towards the main school building.

"Nothing."

Marmalade skipped ahead and started to walk backwards in front of Danny, so he could see his face. "It doesn't look like nothing to me. What's bugging you?" he asked. "And by the way, I'm sorry about the finger in your sandwich earlier."

"Forget it," said Danny. "I'm sorry I snapped at you."

Marmalade spread his hands wide. "S'okay. I can take it. So long as we're still mates."

Danny looked surprised. "Of course."

"Only," Marmalade concentrated on not falling over as he negotiated a corner. "You're not happy, are you?" He slowed right down and Danny had to stop to avoid walking into him.

Danny sighed. "Look. You know what it's like. It's the same for dancers, and musicians and singers. You get given a piece of work that needs a bit of extra slog to get right." A haunted expression passed over his face so quickly that Marmalade wasn't sure he'd really seen it. "And you work extra hard until it comes right."

He bit his lip. "So, if you'll move out of my way I'll get on with the work. Okay with you?" With that, he pushed past Marmalade and strode off down the path.

Marmalade folded his arms and watched his friend go. He had hoped he'd be able to persuade Danny to go to the film that was on in the hall that night, but there didn't seem any chance of that. And there wasn't a lot of point following him. Danny had to be going to the practice rooms, and he'd be even more annoyed if Marmalade hung around while he was trying to work on his drumming. Still, at least they knew what was getting to Danny now.

Marmalade hunched himself into his coat and kept walking. He felt bad that Danny was having trouble, but he knew that getting down in the dumps as well wasn't the answer. Even if Danny wasn't going to the film, Marmalade definitely was. With luck he'd manage to save a place for Tara. He was hoping to slip a huge, squidgy, plastic centipede on the chair without her noticing. He couldn't wait to see the expression on her face when she sat down.

3 A Frustrating Day

Danny stopped drumming and put his sticks on the snare drum. He flexed his fingers and let out his second sigh in as many minutes. He had been practising for ages, and wasn't used to having serious trouble. But over a week ago his drum teacher, Mr. Wright, had demonstrated a particularly difficult piece and then challenged Danny to play it. In the past, however demanding the music, Danny had been able to make at least some progress at the first attempt. But, after spending a whole week wrestling with this rhythm, he was no nearer mastering it than when he'd begun. He'd hoped to celebrate having perfected the piece by his birthday, which was on Sunday, but the way things were going his birthday was going to be just one more day of hard slog and no improvement.

Danny felt so frustrated that he was almost tempted to lash out and kick something. But that wasn't his way. Instead, he tried the piece all over again, only to fail just as badly as before. He gave yet another huge sigh and told himself to calm down. He wouldn't get anywhere trying to play in the mood he was in. He'd have to admit defeat once again, for today at least. Besides, it was late, and he needed to get back to the boys' boarding house.

He forced himself to stand up and stretch, stuffing his drumsticks into his jeans pocket. With one last resentful glance back at his drums, he opened the door of the practice room. All the younger students had left ages ago. Just two girls, final year students, were rehearsing for an audition the following morning. Danny had already wished them luck. They were going for places in a new band and, judging by the quality of their singing, they had to be in with a good chance.

Trick or Treat

Danny didn't have to worry about a career yet, although a few of his friends had already had some success in the music industry. His best friend, Marmalade Stamp, had danced on a pop video and the Lowther twins, Pop and Lolly, had recorded a successful pop song. They were already well-known models, so the song had been the icing on the cake for them.

As Danny made his way along the corridor, he tried to imagine the sorts of problems they faced. How difficult could it be to waft down a catwalk in expensive clothes, or prance about on a video, earning loads of money for doing very little? Compared to the complexity of what he did, they had it easy. Still, he knew in his heart that he wasn't being fair – or even accurate. All his friends worked extremely hard. Part of the skill of performing was to make it look effortless, and Danny was well aware how much practice that took. He was just letting his frustration make him feel sour.

In spite of his disgruntled mood, Danny was generally very pleased with his musical success so far. He had been in the school band – Wizard Monkey Breath Scares the Horses – that had won the International Battle of the Bands competition in Italy. He was enormously proud of that achievement, as were Ed, Ben, Tara and Chloe, who had all performed in the band. And the appearances they had made afterwards had been great fun. But a while ago his drum teacher, Mr. Wright, had told Danny that he shouldn't rush to spend all his time onstage.

"It's fantastic to perform," he'd said. "And I know that's your ultimate ambition. But you don't want to trade good technique for time onstage at your age. You need to give yourself time at school to learn and practise as much as you can. I think you have it in you to be one of the great drummers of your generation. But it takes courage and determination to stick to the hours of practice that requires. Only you can decide what you really want."

Danny did want to be one of the best if he could. But sometimes, like tonight, he began to wonder if all the effort was worth it, especially if he couldn't get his technique right, no matter how hard he tried. He'd missed the film this evening – and it was one he'd had wanted to see for ages – but Danny had told himself that the extra practice would pay off. Well, it hadn't, and now he felt as if he'd missed it for nothing.

He pushed open the swing door to the hall and straight away he could tell that the film had just finished, because lots of students suddenly came pouring in, chattering and laughing about what they'd seen.

"Hi, Danny!" It was Chloe, with most of their friends in tow.

"You should have been there!" said Marmalade, giving Danny a cheeky nudge. "The special effects were awesome!"

"But that's all there was to it," protested Chloe. "The story was feeble! Fun though," she admitted. She grinned at Danny. "How did your practice go? Marmalade said you were tackling a new piece."

Danny shrugged. "Not that new. I've had it nearly a week. And I just can't seem to…"

"Danny, you worry too much," Marmalade smiled

at him encouragingly, "you know you always get it right in the end."

"Not this time," said Danny, feeling as if no one understood. "This time it's different."

"Really?" Chloe could always be relied upon for sympathy. "What a pain for you. What does Mr. Wright say?"

"Oh…don't ask," said Danny, fed up of thinking about it. "I know what I'm *supposed* to do. I just can't manage it. In fact…" His voice wavered and he bit his lip. He didn't want to admit how upset he was, but meeting everyone straight out of the film, with his friends all so happy and laughing, just made him feel worse. "I'm not sure if I'll ever get it right," he said miserably.

"I'm sure you will," said Chloe. "But I know how you feel. I've had tricky times with my voice. Just hang on in there, Danny. It'll come right in the end."

"Chloe's right," said Lolly. "Don't let it get you down."

"Does it have a guitar part to go with it?" asked

Ben. "If so, Ed or I could have a go at playing it for you. That might help…if we could manage it."

"Thanks," said Danny, awkwardly. "But…I'll let you know, okay?"

"Come on, Chloe," said Pop. "Danny's had enough of our sympathy. Let's go back to the boarding house. If you don't come now you'll have to walk back in the dark all by yourself, and…" she gave an extravagant shiver, "anything could be out there, at this time of year!"

"Okay. I'm coming," Chloe laughed.

"We're going back to our house too," said Ben, as they watched the girls make their way out of the main door. "Come on, Danny. There's probably time to play table tennis before bed. Ed and me against you and Marmalade. I've been working at perfecting my topspin. I reckon I'm unbeatable now."

Danny frowned. "That's what practice *should* do, isn't it?" he said. "Make you better at something. But I just feel as if I'm going backwards."

"Forget it for tonight," said Marmalade, throwing his

arm heavily around Danny's shoulders and executing a few intricate dance steps. "That's what I do when I can't get a movement right. You wait. You'll feel much better about it by tomorrow."

"Yeah," said Danny. He felt like throwing off Marmalade's arm, but told himself not to be so irritable. Marmalade was only trying to help. So instead of sounding grumpy, Danny had a go at cheering up for his friends' sake. "Okay," he agreed. "I'll sleep on it and try again tomorrow."

The boys plunged out into the night. The boys' boarding house was in the opposite direction to the girls' house. It was on the far side of the main school building, and all the way past the Rock Department.

It was a rough night, with the wind whooshing through the trees, and there was rain in the wind, darting down at them like cold needles. The boys started running and laughing as the wind got behind them and pushed them along. Danny began to feel better. Perhaps he had been silly to get so depressed about his drumming. Marmalade was right, sleeping on something often made it better. Maybe tomorrow it really would come right straight away. He could always hope.

As soon as they got indoors, Danny shook his head to get rid of the raindrops in his hair.

"Oi! I'm wet enough already!" Marmalade shook his shaggy hair as well, shooting water everywhere.

Danny tried to put drumming to the back of his mind while they played table tennis. Marmalade wasn't the most skilful partner, but he was wildly enthusiastic, and tended to be lucky.

"Look at that!" he boasted as the ball careered off the edge of the table where neither Ed nor Ben could reach it. "Pure skill!"

"Pure luck," grumbled Ed as he retrieved the ball. "Anyway, we're winning."

Ed didn't like to be beaten, and Danny could sympathize with that – not that Danny really cared about losing at table tennis. But he did mind losing at drumming and as he went to bed that night he told himself that he wouldn't allow himself to be beaten.

A Frustrating Day

Tomorrow he'd get up early and fit in an extra practice, in fact he'd fit in as many as he could, every day, until he'd got that piece of drum music thoroughly sorted. Failure wasn't an option.

4 Chloe and Danny

Early the next morning, Danny was woken by the sun streaming in through a gap in the curtains. The storm had blown itself out and it looked as if it was going to be a brilliant autumn day. Danny sat up and looked at the still-sleeping figures in the other three beds. Marmalade, Ed and Ben never liked getting up early, but Danny had always enjoyed the first part of the day. Even so, it was *very* early, and he was tempted to turn over and go back to sleep. But he had decided the previous night to put in as many extra practices as possible, so he slid quietly out of bed.

Once he was dressed, he went downstairs and opened the front door. Outside it was chilly, but the sky was clear and he wanted to be out. He wasn't ready to shut himself into a practice room just yet and he fancied a walk round the lake. He knew he could do that and still have a bit of time to practise before breakfast. He dragged his mobile out of his pocket and texted Chloe. It would be nice to have company, if she was awake.

The lake was quite big, and on the far side there were several large trees, though most had bare branches at this time of the year. Danny scuffed his way through the damp, fallen leaves, enjoying the rhythm of his walk and thinking how the sound the leaves made was like some sort of natural percussion instrument around his feet. As he headed round the top of the lake and made his way towards the bench on the lawn outside the main school building, he saw a figure approaching from the direction of the girls' boarding house. It was Chloe. She reached the bench before he did, and sat down to wait for him.

"Hello! I thought you must still be asleep when you didn't text back."

Chloe grinned. "I thought I'd surprise you. I was just getting up actually when I got your message. I like to do my voice exercises outside in the mornings, if I can, and today was too good an opportunity to miss." She took a deep breath and soared up through the scales. Danny sat and listened. He was always astonished by Chloe's huge voice. He loved listening to her warming up.

"So, how are you this morning?" she asked as soon as she'd finished. "You sounded so fed up last night."

"I thought I felt a bit better today," said Danny. "But now I'm not so sure. I seem to be losing my confidence, but I'm going to go and practise in a minute. I reckon I've just got to keep working at it."

"So what is it you're finding so difficult?"

"Well," said Danny, pleased that Chloe was interested. "It's like this. You know how I have to use both hands and both feet for the drum kit?"

Chloe nodded. "I don't know how you do it," she said.

"It's okay if you can move everything to the same

rhythm," he explained. "Why don't you have a go? You don't need a drum kit to try it." He began tapping both feet on the ground at the same time and Chloe did the same. Then he added both hands, tapping gently on his knee.

"I can do that!" said Chloe.

"Now, try the basic drum beat every drummer learns," said Danny. "Let your right hand carry on tapping – one, two, three, four – while your right foot just taps on the one."

After a few fumbles Chloe shot Danny a triumphant grin. "Like that! Oops, talking to you made me mess up."

Danny smiled. "Keep it going. Now add in your left hand. It has to go one two three, one two three, one two three."

No matter how she tried, Chloe couldn't do it. "It's impossible!" she said.

Danny replied by tapping the three different sets of beats for her effortlessly. It made her head spin. "That's fantastic," she said. "No matter how much I practised I know I could never do that, Danny. You're so clever."

"But I've just been showing you the simplest rhythm," he said. "It gets much more complicated than that."

Chloe clutched her head. "Don't!"

"The thing is," he told her. "The new piece I'm trying to learn mixes it all up. Instead of the right hand counting four, it's my left foot that has to do that. And my right hand has to count the second and fourth beats instead of the classic four. The left hand is okay. It's still on the third beat, but the bass drum – that's my right foot – well..." He shook his head. "It's all over the place. I can play it fine on its own, but no matter how hard I try I just can't put all four together." Sitting on the bench he tried again, remembering the rhythms of the drum music his teacher had given him. He had the high hat and ride cymbal perfectly, and with his left hand he could play the snare drum correctly too, but every time he brought in his right foot to play the complicated bass drum part, his brain couldn't cope.

"It's no good," he said, throwing himself back on the bench and staring up into the pale blue sky. "I'm *never* going to get it right."

Chloe sat quietly by his side. "You have to believe in yourself," she said at last. "Remember that time I lost my voice? I'd lost faith in myself then, and nothing worked for me. If you get scared it makes it so much harder."

Danny looked at her, his eyes full of pain. "I know," he said, sounding choked up. "And I'm trying not to be, but I *am* afraid, of several things. I'm afraid I'm going to lose my friends if I stay this miserable. Marmalade was only having a laugh yesterday, and I almost bit his head off. And Chloe, I don't want to sound melodramatic, but what if this is as far as I can go with my drumming?"

For a few seconds there was silence. Chloe couldn't think what to say. Things were great for her at the moment. Her voice was improving all the time, and it was exciting to wonder just what she might be capable of in the future. It would be awful if she thought she'd gone as far as she could. She put out her hand to comfort him, but Danny stood up. He didn't say anything, but turned and started running. She watched him go with a worried expression on her face. He really was in a bad way. Chloe wished she could do or say *something* to make him feel better. She hadn't even had a chance to reassure him about his friends.

She stayed where she was for a while, thinking about Danny. Then she got up with a determined look on her face. Danny needed help. His friends might not be able to do anything about his drumming, but surely they could rally round and make him feel better about himself? Chloe wasn't sure how, but there had to be something they could do. For a start everyone ought to know that this was more than a little problem that would soon go away. Danny was struggling, and it was no good his friends trying to make light of it. That would just make him feel worse. She had to get everyone together while he wasn't around so they could decide what to do. Danny needed to know that his friends weren't going to desert him just because he was struggling, and not joining in with them.

Chloe headed straight to the main school building. She wondered if the dining room was open yet. She was hungry, and she couldn't wait to meet the others to put some sort of plan in place to help Danny. Surely, between them, her friends would be able to think of *something*.

5 Operation Danny

Every school day at Rockley Park was packed full of lessons and activities, and this one was no exception. However much Chloe wanted to tell her friends about her chat with Danny, whenever she tried to mention it, either he was there, or several people were missing – off at their individual music lessons, or busy with one project or another. So Chloe decided to wait until she was back in her room with Tara, Pop and Lolly. At least she could be sure Danny wouldn't suddenly turn up there.

Having been thwarted all day long, as soon as the four girls were in their room at the end of the day, Chloe was ready to burst. She flung herself on her bed and gave a huge sigh. "Thank goodness!"

"What's up with you?" said Tara, pulling a comb through her short, black hair.

"I've been waiting to talk to you all day about Danny!" said Chloe. "I saw him this morning and asked what was wrong. Well, his problem is much more serious than we thought. He really needs help!"

"Tell all," said Lolly. "You know we'll do whatever we can."

"Well, I don't think he's ever struggled so much with his drumming," explained Chloe. "He seems to have hit a wall, and is scared he might not be able to get any further."

Pop frowned. "If you'd asked me last week which one of us would struggle the most I would *never* have said Danny. He's *soo* talented."

Tara nodded. "I'd have said the same. But I suppose the better you are, the harder it seems if you start to lose faith in yourself…"

"And the better you are the more people demand of you," added Lolly.

"Maybe he needs to take a step back," said Pop uncertainly.

"Well we can't advise him about his drumming," said Tara. "But if we could just take his mind off his worries for a bit, surely that would help?"

"That's exactly what I was thinking," said Chloe. "But how? He's also worrying that because he's such poor company at the moment his friends will desert him."

"That's stupid," said Pop.

"But he's feeling so bad about himself he can't see that." Chloe was feeling more and more upset for her friend.

"I know what," said Lolly.

Chloe, Tara and Pop looked up hopefully, but Lolly shook her head. "It's not a brilliant plan, but I'm sure once we have a chance to discuss it properly with Ed, Ben and Marmalade as well we're *bound* to come up with something. We know they're just as concerned about Danny as we are. He's not about to lose his friends. Of course we're here for him. So all we have to do is think of something that'll make him believe it."

"Okay." Chloe looked at Lolly and nodded her head firmly. "You're right."

She got up and gave the three girls a hug. "Thanks," she said. "I'm lucky to have you to help."

Lolly gave her a big hug in return. "And Danny is lucky that you care about him so much."

Over at the boys' boarding house, Marmalade was trying to take Danny's mind off his worries in his own way.

"Danny, mate, I need a hand," he muttered as they arrived back at the house.

"What with?" asked Danny.

"Ssh." Marmalade grabbed Danny's shoulder and held him back, while Ben and Ed disappeared indoors. "I'm going to play a great trick on Ed and Ben, but it wouldn't be fair to trick you again, so I need you to be in on it instead." He explained about his pledge to trick everyone before Halloween.

Danny sighed. "So what do you want me to do?" he said.

Trick or Treat

"It'll be a laugh," said Marmalade encouragingly. "I'm going to make the bedroom door keep opening when we're in bed after lights out. It'll annoy the socks off them. And all you have to do is be a lookout while I set it up. Don't let the secret out."

"How are you going to do it?" said Danny, getting interested in spite of himself.

"Simple," said Marmalade. "All you need is some screwed-up paper and a bit of thread."

Danny frowned. "Really?"

Mr. South, the boys' housemaster, was doing his rounds. He always checked the rooms at lights out, to make sure everyone was in bed and ready to sleep.

"Night lads," he said, and closed the door behind him. For a few seconds after he'd gone, all was quiet, but then the door started to swing open, and light from the corridor shone onto Ben's face. Ben frowned. He knew the light would stop him from sleeping. Reluctantly he got up.

"The door didn't close properly," he grumbled. He lunged at the offending door and pushed it back into place. But as soon as he was settled back in bed the door swung open again.

"Ha, ha!" laughed Ed. "Now *you* haven't shut it."

Ben jumped out of bed and gave the door an almighty shove. He glared at it angrily, but it seemed to have latched okay this time. He went back to his bed and lifted the duvet, ready to slide underneath, then turned and gave the door one last hard look. It was still shut.

For a few minutes everyone was quiet as they settled down to sleep at last, but just as Ben was beginning to drift off, the offending door began to open once more, with an irritating creak.

"Ben!" Ed sat up in bed and glared at Ben. Marmalade was trying to keep his laughter under control, but it was very difficult. Even Danny was smiling.

Ben turned over in bed and groaned. "I *did* shut it. You do it if you're so clever."

Trick or Treat

Ed got out of bed and padded over to the door. Instead of shoving it, like Ben had, he took hold of the door handle carefully. He started to close it, then hesitated. "There's some thread tied to the door handle."

No one replied, but Marmalade hastily dropped the end of the thread that he'd been holding and tried to pretend he was asleep.

Ed now had the door almost closed. He tried latching it gently, but every time he pulled the handle it opened again. "Why isn't it closing properly?" he muttered to himself. "It usually does."

"Hurry up, won't you?" said Ben. "I want to get to sleep."

"Hang on a minute." Ed switched on the light and everybody started to complain loudly. But now, Ed could see that the other end of the thread ended suspiciously by Marmalade's bed. He must have been using it to pull the door open. And Ed could also see that someone had stuffed paper into the latch so that the door couldn't close properly.

"I admit it!" said Marmalade, ducking as a horde of slippers, paperbacks and clothes rained down on him from both Ed and Ben. "But you must admit," he added, throwing a slipper back to Ben. "It was a pretty good trick!"

6 Marmalade's Plan

The next morning at breakfast the boys were still laughing at Marmalade's trick when the girls arrived.

"How do you dream up these ideas?" said Chloe with a giggle.

"My granny told me about the door one," said Marmalade. "She must have been *terrible* when she was young."

"See you later," said Danny, getting up from the table.

"It's ages before first lesson," said Chloe in surprise. "Aren't you staying to chat?"

Danny looked at her. "I told you yesterday," he said. "I have to keep trying." Without another word he picked up his tray, dumped it in the rack and left.

"Oh dear," said Lolly.

"He's still not happy, is he?" said Pop.

"No," Marmalade agreed. "I thought last night might have cheered him up, but nothing we do seems to make any difference."

Chloe quickly explained to the boys how serious Danny's worries were. "And as if that wasn't enough," she went on, "it's his birthday on Sunday. I bet he won't be in any sort of mood to celebrate. You know how sometimes, when you're down because things are going wrong, even a birthday doesn't cheer you up."

Lolly and Tara nodded, but Marmalade looked impatient. "Well that's easy!" he said. "Let's give him a surprise party on Sunday night. Think about it. You're miserable, life seems horrible, and you're not even looking forward to your birthday...but your friends throw you a surprise birthday party to show you what a great person you are. You'd have to be crazy not to be cheered up by that!"

Trick or Treat

Chloe couldn't help smiling at Marmalade's enthusiasm. "Well, it would take his mind off his troubles, for a while at least," she agreed. "And it would make him feel special too. If that doesn't reassure him about his friends I don't know what will. Let's go for it!"

"A party is a great idea," Ed agreed. "We could have a Halloween theme with cobwebs and plastic bats and people dressed up as Dracula and witches and..."

"That sounds fun," said Lolly. Then she looked doubtful. "But where could we hold it?"

"Why don't we ask Judge Jim if we can have it in the Rock Department?" said Ben.

"That's a great idea!" Chloe smiled at him. "It's the perfect size for our year group, and music won't be a problem. Who's going to ask him?"

"I will," said Tara. "I have a bass lesson with him later."

"Great," said Pop, her eyes shining. "I love parties, especially ones where we can dress up. And we'll be cheering Danny up too. How perfect is that?"

On their way out of the dining room after breakfast, a couple of students from year seven approached them. "Can I ask you something?" one said, looking rather shy.

"Of course," said Chloe. "What can we do to help? It's Colby, isn't it? You and Brooke share a room, don't you?"

They looked pleased that Chloe knew their names. "I just wanted to ask about the ghost," said Colby.

Tara rolled her eyes.

"Only, Brooke thought she saw it last night, at the far end of the practice-rooms corridor. Isn't that right, Brooke?"

The slim girl loitering nearby nodded. "It was sort of jerking along," she explained, waving her arms to demonstrate. "And it didn't make any sort of noise."

"Well," Chloe smiled. "It *is* nearly Halloween. Lots of students like dressing up and playing tricks at this time of year. I expect that's what you saw, Brooke. None of us has ever seen a ghost, have we?" She looked at her friends and they all shook their heads.

"But," said Colby, earnestly. "Doesn't it appear to someone when something terrible is going to happen? That's what Charlie said." She shivered.

"Don't take any notice of him," said Lolly kindly. "I don't believe in ghosts, whatever Charlie might say."

"Nor me," said Tara firmly.

"Me neither," said Chloe.

Brooke and Colby looked at Pop and she shrugged.

"Trust Charlie to scare the younger ones," said Tara, once Colby and Brooke had gone. "As if they need any encouragement."

Pop and Lolly wanted to make a quick visit to the library, while Chloe headed to lessons with Tara. After a few minutes Danny arrived. He tucked his drumsticks into his backpack and sat down glumly.

"How did your practice go this morning?" asked Chloe.

Danny frowned. "I'm getting worse instead of better," he said. "That's never happened before." He stared gloomily into space for a moment and then sighed.

"Never mind." He picked up a book and flipped through it. It was obvious that he did mind very much indeed.

Chloe couldn't think of anything to say. In all the time she'd known him she'd never seen Danny look so defeated. She looked at Tara, but Tara was obviously out of ideas too.

Danny sighed, and pushed the book away from him. "I'll have another practice later," he said. He was trying to put a brave face on things, but he certainly didn't fool her.

It was quite a relief when some of the other students came in and began chatting normally. Things improved a bit more when Marmalade arrived and sat at the back, wearing a horrible Halloween mask. He was so still and quiet that it was quite a few minutes before the teacher noticed, and by that time all the students were in hysterics.

7 A Scare for Danny

Danny didn't go to practice straight after lessons. Even he recognized that he needed a bit of a break at the end of the school day, and there was homework to be done as well. Just because the school existed to help its students make it in the music business, didn't mean academic subjects weren't important too. So Danny went back to the house, made himself a drink and a snack, and relaxed for half an hour before homework and tea. After tea, however, the rest of the evening was his, and he spent every moment of that time at his drum kit in the main house, in one of the special practice rooms.

He didn't join his friends for an evening jam session

in the Rock Department, or play table tennis or watch TV. But however hard he worked, he kept getting worse instead of better. Even rhythms he had always managed perfectly well were becoming more difficult to get right. He came in late, fluffed his rim shots, and was even dropping his sticks far more than he ever used to.

He was deep in thought as he left his practice room and headed up the long corridor that led to the main part of the building and the way out. It was a very quiet time of night, and the corridor was quite gloomy. But up at the end, near the door, a grey, ragged-looking figure suddenly appeared in the gloom. Its movements were strange and jerky, disturbingly like a life-sized puppet, twitching on the end of its strings. Then it disappeared again. Danny wasn't sure whether it had actually gone through the door or quite simply vanished. He hesitated. The figure had looked distinctly weird. Danny felt a disturbing tremor trickle up his spine. All of a sudden he didn't feel very happy about walking down the corridor any more, but if he wanted to leave the building it was the only way out. Behind him was a dead end. He stuffed his hands in his pockets and told himself not to be so stupid. There had to be a sensible explanation. Probably he'd been concentrating for too long. His eyes certainly felt tired. No doubt it was some other student going home late, or even the caretaker. Nothing weird about that at all.

He carried on walking, and soon reached the door. There was nothing there; nothing to be scared about at all. He walked through into the deserted hallway. The sweeping staircase rose up to his right, and the large front door was ahead of him. Rockley Park House was very old, and he supposed it could feel a bit spooky at times. But he reminded himself that there really was nothing there.

He pushed open the door and went outside. There was a bit of mist rising, and it was chilly. He hunched into his jacket and headed towards his boarding house, past the Rock Department, now all in darkness, and round the corner. He was just telling himself how silly he had been to feel unsettled when there was a rustling in the bushes to his right. Before he had a chance to look, something horrible leaped out in front of him.

Danny let out a yelp and stumbled backwards. The thing had a ghastly green face, with blood dripping from its mouth and bloodshot eyes that dangled from their sockets.

It was only as the thing had darted away, with a blood-curdling chuckle, that Danny realized he'd been had. The boy wearing the mask had been too short to be Marmalade. For once this wasn't one of *his* tricks. It had to be one of the younger students; David probably. He was almost as much of a tease as Marmalade, and seemed to take a special delight in playing tricks on the older boys. No doubt he'd soon be boasting to his friends about how he'd scared Danny James. Danny didn't mind that, but he really wasn't in the mood for jokes, especially the sort that made his heart race so fast. His nerves were already jangling as it was.

As soon as he got indoors he hung up his coat and went in search of a drink. "Hi!" he said to Ed, who was coming out of the kitchen with a steaming mug of hot chocolate in his hand. "Is there enough hot water left for another of those?" He shivered. "I could really do with one."

"What's up with you?" asked Ed. "Are you all right?"

"I'm okay," said Danny. "Just a bit fed up."

"Thank goodness," said Ed, punching him lightly on his shoulder. "I was afraid you'd seen the ghost! You know," he added, seeing that Danny wasn't following his meaning, "the one that's supposed to walk the corridors at Halloween. Charlie has been scaring the younger students, telling them it only appears when something dreadful is about to happen." He laughed. "Chloe told me some of the younger girls are really spooked. They think they've seen it! I reckon the boys aren't daft enough to believe in it, though."

"No," said Danny, feeling another shiver trickle up his spine. "I don't suppose they are."

Over in the girls' house, Tara was telling her roommates about her meeting with Judge Jim.

"It was brilliant!" she told Chloe, Pop and Lolly. "He

said yes straight away. He thought a Halloween birthday party was a great idea. And when I mentioned that we'd like to keep it a secret from Danny he said that he was good at keeping secrets, so if it got out we weren't to blame him!"

"That's so cool!" said Chloe happily. "A Halloween birthday party in the Rock Department. What could be better?"

"We'll have to sort out some spooky decorations," said Lolly. "I wonder if we can get permission to go into town on the bus tomorrow afternoon?"

"We can ask Mrs. Pinto," said Chloe, "when she comes in at lights out. I expect she'll let us."

"I fancy going as a witch, with a tall black hat and long black nails," said Pop. "It would be fun shopping for the costumes. And we need to get a present for Danny, of course."

"This is going to be the one occasion when you *don't* try to get me to wear something more colourful," said Tara with great satisfaction, looking down at her top and jeans, which were black as always. Her pale

Trick or Treat

face and dark clothes looked great when she was playing bass with Ed and Ben on guitar and Danny on drums, but the twins were always trying to get her to brighten herself up on other occasions.

Lolly laughed. "You're right," she said. "In fact I may even be forced to ask if I can borrow one of your tops. Apart from one pair of trousers I don't think I have anything black in my whole wardrobe."

"I can't believe that!" said Chloe. "It's bulging."

"Let's have a look," said Pop, bouncing over to the wardrobe and throwing it open.

By the time Mrs. Pinto came in, their beds were piled high with a jumble of clothes.

"What a mess!" she scolded. "How are you going to get to bed like that?"

"We forgot what the time was," said Lolly, sweeping an armful of clothes off her bed and bundling them into the bottom of her wardrobe. "Sorry."

Chloe explained about the surprise party on Sunday night, and asked about going into town the next afternoon. Mrs. Pinto agreed right away. "As long as you clear all these clothes up and put them away *tidily*," she insisted, giving the heap in the wardrobe a hard stare.

"I expect you'll be able to borrow some props from the wardrobe department," she added. "You can have a look tomorrow. And if you like I'll speak to the kitchen staff about food. I'm sure they'll be happy to let you have some party nibbles."

The girls went to bed in very high spirits.

"I don't know about cheering Danny up, but I'm having fun," said Pop as she scrambled into bed.

"He's going to love it when he finds out," said Chloe confidently. "Only two days to go! I can't wait to see Danny's face when he arrives to find us all dressed up, and the Rock Department decorated." Then she hesitated. "Do you think the whole year can keep it secret until Sunday?"

8 Danny Alone

Danny got up on Saturday morning determined to be more cheerful in front of his friends, but at breakfast, when Chloe asked him how he was feeling, he couldn't help but be honest.

"I don't know what I'm going to do," he told her. "I've run out of ideas. The harder I practise the worse I get, and I know I'm not easy to be with at the moment. I keep moaning on far too much."

"Oh Danny," said Chloe. "Stop thinking that we won't like you because you're down. That's just not true. And look, why don't you take a break from your drums this weekend? It can't do any harm, and it might even do you some good. You never know." She looked urgently into his face and Danny's heart turned over. She was his oldest friend and suddenly he realized how special she was. She believed in him as a person. He got the feeling that, even if he never played drums again, she'd still like him just as much.

Danny put his hand on her sleeve and squeezed her arm.

"Thanks," he said. "Maybe I *should* take a break. What are you doing this afternoon?"

Chloe's face fell. "Um, well, I have to go into town with Pop and Lolly," she said. "Otherwise I'd suggest we did something together."

"Oh, it doesn't matter," said Danny, disappointed that Chloe hadn't asked if he wanted to go into town too. "I'll spend the afternoon with Marmalade."

"Good idea!" Chloe sounded relieved. "He'll keep you smiling. Come on. We must get to lessons."

In her determination to make helpful suggestions for Danny, Chloe had forgotten about the party arrangements. Now she was worried. What if he gave up practising all over the weekend? They had assumed he would be occupied while they organized the party!

After lessons, and on the way to lunch, Danny asked Marmalade if he'd like to play a computer game with him that afternoon. Marmalade looked awkward.

"Sorry, mate," he said after a pause. "Er, I promised some of the senior dancers that I'd help out with a project they're doing."

"Oh. Maybe I could come along and watch?" said Danny hopefully. "If I promised not to get in the way. I like dance rehearsals."

Marmalade looked anxious and shook his head vigorously. "It's much too early in the project for spectators," he told Danny. "They wouldn't be happy. And they are seniors. I have to do what they say, don't I?"

"Yes, you're right," Danny agreed, but he couldn't shake off the feeling that Marmalade was keeping something from him. "Never mind. It doesn't matter." But it did matter to Danny. He was afraid that Marmalade was making excuses not to spend time with him, and the thought made him even more miserable.

Danny Alone

On his way back to his room after lunch, Danny passed a group of boys from his year having a kick about with a football. He could have asked to join in, but he didn't. If they wanted him surely they'd have asked? Nobody wanted to do anything with him. Even Ben and Ed had disappeared; Danny couldn't find them anywhere.

In spite of Chloe's reassuring words, Danny couldn't help feeling that people were avoiding him. Maybe they had all got so used to him spending every spare moment practising recently they just assumed he didn't want to spend time with them any more. Well, he supposed that had been true. And if it hadn't been for Chloe's suggestion to take a break from drumming he'd have been in the practice room again right now.

He went to his bedroom, but no one was there. Downstairs a couple of people were watching a TV programme that he hated. For a moment Danny hesitated, not sure what to do. Then he slung on his jacket, picked up his drumsticks and headed back to his drum kit.

Trick or Treat

As soon as he got into the dim practice-rooms corridor, he felt the same shiver running up his spine that he'd felt before. It was daylight outside, but in this part of the old house there was no natural light. He peered into the gloom ahead of him. Right at the end of the corridor it looked as if someone was there, standing motionless in the dark. It had to be the same, odd-looking figure that he'd seen before.

Danny halted. Suddenly he didn't feel like practising any more. He turned round and saw the strange figure at the *other* end of the corridor, blocking his escape. How on earth had it got past him?

He told himself not to be stupid, but he couldn't help it. He panicked, fumbling for his mobile to call for help. But there was never a signal down here. He looked up again and it seemed to him as if the figure was walking towards him. He turned again and ran back to his practice room. Once inside he closed the door and stood there alone, waiting.

✳

As soon as Mrs. Pinto brought the car to the door the girls all piled in, chattering excitedly about what they were going to buy for the party.

"Thanks for giving us a lift," said Lolly.

"We'd have had to wait ages for the bus," added Chloe.

"You're welcome," said Mrs. Pinto, as she pulled out onto the main road. "I had to go into town anyway." She parked at the shopping mall, and they arranged a time to meet back at the car.

The girls had a lot of fun shopping. First, they got a huge bundle of cobwebby decorations that would look great draped over the Rock Department speakers, and dangled around the room. At the same shop they bought some plastic bats and a string of party lights shaped like pumpkins. To complete the decorations they bought a large, blow-up ghost. Then they found a witch's hat each, and one for Tara, who had opted to stay behind and help Ed and Ben sort out the party music.

"I'm sure she'll love it," said Pop.

Trick or Treat

They got sets of plastic talons to wear over the ends of their fingers, and found a huge banner that said "Happy Birthday".

"We have to have that!" said Chloe. "Do we have enough money?"

"Yes," said Lolly, looking in her purse.

Chloe already had a card for Danny, so Pop and Lolly bought him one between them. Then they all joined together to buy a huge pack of Halloween sweets as a birthday present.

As they went past the baker's on the way home, Chloe spotted a cake with marzipan pumpkins on. "The perfect birthday cake!" she squealed.

"Let's get some of those trick candles too. You know, the ones that are almost impossible to blow out!" said Pop. So they did.

Meanwhile, Danny waited in the practice room. He was trapped. There was nowhere else to go, no lock on the door, and nothing to barricade it with. His heart was thumping in his chest. He tried to breathe more slowly. He had to stay calm and listen.

But there was no sound in the corridor and the minutes ticked by. *I can't stay here for ever*, he thought. He chanced a glance out of the door. The corridor was deserted in both directions. He grabbed his drumsticks and ran towards the exit. When he got to the door he looked back. The corridor was still empty.

The hall was buzzing, however. A group of senior students was waiting for a lift to the local bowling alley, some girls in the year above Danny had laid on a pop quiz, and there was going to be a film for the younger students. But none of his friends was involved in any of that.

"Are you all right?" Two young girls were standing by the stairs, looking at him.

"You look as if you've seen a ghost," said one.

Danny tried to smile, but it wasn't a great success. "What makes you say that?"

"You look like Brooke did when she saw it."

The other girl nodded. "It gave me a huge shock.

That's why we're not going to the film tonight. It's too spooky for us."

"Where did you see this ghost?" said Danny, trying to sound casual.

Brooke pointed to the door Danny had just emerged from. "Going through there."

Danny's back prickled. But Brooke wasn't taking any notice of him. She was looking up.

"Colby!" Brooke was staring up at the top of the stairs.

Danny and Colby followed her gaze, and Danny caught a glimpse of something grey and ragged disappearing jerkily into a doorway on the landing. Colby and Brooke looked at each other and then at Danny.

"That was it." Colby sounded pleased. "That was the ghost."

On the way back to the car the girls noticed some real pumpkins in a greengrocer's shop and bought a big one. Chloe was staggering along with it when her phone buzzed.

"Here, give me that," said Lolly.

Chloe dug her phone out of her bag and read out the text she had just received. "It's Danny," she said, looking puzzled. "He wants me to meet him in the hall. He says it's urgent."

"I wonder what's happened?" said Lolly.

"I don't know," Chloe was texting busily. "But we should be back in about half an hour. I've said I'll meet him then."

On the journey home in the car the girls tried on their hats. "I think we ought to haunt the boys tonight," said Pop.

"Especially Marmalade!" said Lolly, with a laugh. "I wonder what he's up to?"

"I'll text him," said Pop. In a few minutes she had a text back. "He's going to the Rock Department to meet Ben and Ed," she said gleefully. "They found some good things for the party in the props department and he's helping sort them out. I reckon when we're ready we should text Ben to send Marmalade outside. It's already getting dark. We can hide in the bushes and jump out at him!"

Back at school, Mrs. Pinto dropped Chloe at the main house, before taking Pop, Lolly and all their shopping on to the boarding house.

"See you later," said Chloe, getting out of the car. "Have fun with the haunting."

"Have fun with Danny," said Lolly. "I hope whatever was urgent is urgent in a good way."

"Me too," said Chloe, feeling a bit anxious. "I hope he's okay. Surely he can't have had anything else go wrong in his life?"

9 Hauntings

Danny had listened to everything Brooke and Colby told him about the Rockley Park ghost. Whilst the two young girls seemed rather to enjoy being spooked, he took it much more seriously. He wasn't convinced that the figure they had glimpsed together *was* a ghost but he felt sure that alone in the corridor he'd seen something he couldn't explain. And, he hated to admit it even to himself, but whatever it was had definitely scared him.

Brooke and Colby soon disappeared off to meet their friends and, while Danny waited for Chloe, he sat down to think.

Maybe he had spent too much time alone, stressing about his drumming failure. Brooding was bad for you.

Trick or Treat

Marmalade was always telling him that. Could he have imagined the strange figure in the corridor because he was stressed out? It didn't seem very likely. Well, what if the ghost *was* real, and *did* appear to warn people about a coming disaster? Danny felt that his drumming was getting worse the more he practised instead of better. What if he lost his ability to drum at all, just because he was overdoing it? Was that the disaster the ghost was warning him away from?

Danny didn't like believing in ghosts, but maybe if he gave up obsessing about his drumming the haunting would stop. He imagined telling Mr. Wright that he couldn't manage the piece. It wouldn't be the end of the world. His teacher might be surprised, but he wouldn't be cross. That wasn't his way. All in all, Danny hated to admit it, but perhaps he needed to accept that he'd failed this time, and move on.

He saw Chloe as soon as she entered the hall and rushed over to greet her.

"Sorry I couldn't come sooner," she said. "We've only just got back."

"That's okay. Was it a good shopping trip?"

"Fine thanks. But what did you want that was so urgent?"

"I've been doing some serious thinking, Chloe. I've decided to give up on that drumming piece. I'm going to tell Mr. Wright it's too hard."

She stared at him. "Wow, Danny! That's quite a decision." She hesitated. "And I think it's a brave one. You've never wanted to give up on anything before. Are you okay about it?"

Danny nodded. "Yes. I think so. It's the right thing to do." He wondered about saying more to her. He really wanted to tell her about the haunting, but couldn't quite bring himself to do it. "I've been neglecting my friends," he said. "And in the end they're just as important. So. Tomorrow." He looked anxiously at her. "Are you going to be busy all day, or can we hang out together for a while?"

Chloe's brain started racing. She thought about all the things they needed to do before Danny's surprise party. They had to decorate the Rock Department, sort out their costumes, turn the pumpkin into a lantern, fetch the food and put it out... How would they manage? But in spite of all that she was sure he'd made the right decision for him. And his friends couldn't desert him on his birthday, when he was trying so hard to sort himself out. She just had to think of something to keep him away from the Rock Department until they were ready for him.

"Pumpkin!" she said.

"What?"

"We bought a pumpkin to make into a lantern. Would you like to help? You know how hard they are to scrape out."

Danny smiled. "That would be great! When?"

"Um...I'm not sure," she said. "I'll need to talk to the others. But look, why don't you come with me now? Pop and Lolly are going to trick Marmalade. If we hurry we might be in time to join in."

"Okay," said Danny. "It'll be quite something if they can get one over on Marmalade!"

They went outside together. Chloe texted Lolly and

got a reply right back. "They're this side of the Rock Department," she told Danny. "We need to hurry."

It was beginning to get foggy. The fog muffled their voices and their footsteps, and made every bush and tree loom suddenly out of the dark. Then, by the light from a lamppost near the Rock Department they could clearly see three figures wearing tall, pointed hats. "There they are," said Chloe with a laugh. "Don't they look good?" She grabbed Danny's arm and they hurried to join the witches, but as they drew close Chloe squealed, and Danny pulled away from the girls in alarm.

"What on earth have you got on your faces?" said Chloe, recovering quickly from her fright. "You look terrifying!"

"It's a white face mask Pop had," said Lolly. "Don't you think it looks good? Hi, Danny, are you okay?"

Danny nodded, trying to still his thudding heart. He was annoyed with himself for getting spooked so easily, but the weird, white faces had reminded him of the figure he'd seen in the practice-rooms corridor.

"It's horrible," Chloe told the twins with a laugh. "Is Marmalade still in the Rock Department with Ed and Ben?"

Tara nodded. "And they're going to send him out as soon as Pop texts again." She held something out to Chloe. "Thanks for getting me a hat by the way. They look great. We brought yours in case you wanted to join us." She hesitated and looked at Danny. "Sorry. We don't have one for you."

Danny shrugged. "It doesn't matter."

"You can still hide with us, Danny," said Lolly. "Come on."

As they all crouched in amongst the wet, prickly bushes that lined the path they couldn't help giggling. Lolly lit up her face with the green light from a torch, which made them giggle even more. Then, Pop texted Ben and they all waited, holding their breath. Danny was squashed close to Chloe. She turned to look at him and their noses almost touched. "Okay?" she whispered.

"Okay," he replied. She smiled at him and he smiled back. "Chloe…"

"Shush," said Pop. "Link hands so we all jump up together. He's coming."

The door of the Rock Department slammed, and a Marmalade-shaped figure loomed out of the fog. He was coming down the path, all by himself. Pop grabbed Danny's hand and Danny took Chloe's and held it tight. Marmalade was whistling. He didn't seem to have a care in the world. But they soon changed that. As he drew level with the bushes they all leaped up, yelling and howling. Marmalade yelped, stumbled backwards and almost fell over.

"Got you!" shouted Tara, triumphantly.

"Rubbish," said Marmalade, recovering quickly, although he looked pretty shaken. "I knew you were there. I could see your hats."

"Yeah, right," said Pop. "We were really well hidden, and besides, you can't see anything in this fog."

"I can see you've got something on your faces," said Marmalade, coming closer, and peering at Pop. "Whatever is it? It looks as if your face is cracking."

"It is," said Pop, leering at him.

Ed and Ben came out to join them and they all had a good laugh at Marmalade's expense. "All right," he admitted at last. "You got me good and proper. And I probably deserved it. Let's go and get some tea. I'm starving."

On the way, Danny told them about his decision to abandon the complicated drumming and spend more time with them. He had assumed they'd be pleased, and he wasn't at all prepared for their reactions.

"Are you sure?" said Pop.

"Don't you want to give it one more go tomorrow?" said Ben.

"Sunday is a good day for practising," said Tara. "Because there aren't any normal lessons. You could spend all day at it."

"Well if you don't *want* me around," said Danny, feeling as if whatever he did it was wrong. He felt like saying, *But it's my birthday!*

Chloe and Marmalade exchanged awkward glances.

"What is it?" said Danny. "You could at least tell me if you don't want to include me in whatever you're doing."

"No!" said Lolly. "It's not that."

"I asked you to help me with our pumpkin," said Chloe, hastily.

"And anything you want to do from Monday onwards, I'm your man," said Marmalade.

Danny looked resigned. "But it's obvious you don't want to spend time with me tomorrow," he muttered.

10 Happy Birthday?

No one got up particularly early on a Sunday. It was the only day of the week when they could have a bit of a lie in, and most people took advantage of that. Usually, Danny, Ed, Ben and Marmalade played computer games together on a Sunday morning, and a bit of football for a while in the afternoon if the weather was fine. The rest of the time was spent in the Rock Department, making music.

Today, things were very different. Danny wondered what on earth he was he going to do with himself. He tried to feel relieved that he wasn't going to struggle with his drumming any more, but his fingers were twitching, dying to pick up his sticks. How could he get through the day?

Danny had never felt in less of a birthday mood, but he did have several cards and a parcel by his bed. They had come in the post, and he had saved them for today.

He always tended to wake early, and today was no exception. His roommates were still sleeping, as usual. But then, Marmalade's phone bleeped and Danny watched with some amusement as Marmalade reached out and fumbled for it.

"Yeah? Yeah…um…okay…yeah." Marmalade mumbled, before putting the phone down. He stretched hugely and sat up, looking even more tousled than usual. He yawned and ran his hands through his bright ginger hair, and then noticed that Danny was awake. "Ah…Sunday. Don't you just love it?" he said. "Except when you have to get up early." He swung his feet to the floor and yawned again.

Danny felt startled. "Get up early? You? What for?" he asked.

Marmalade seemed to be searching sleepily for a

believable reply. "Well…more stuff to do with the senior dancers. You know how it is." He busied himself with searching under the bed for his slippers, then padded off to the bathroom.

"Oh. Right," Danny said, quietly.

When Marmalade came back Danny was still in bed, staring up at the ceiling.

"I expect I'll be finished by lunchtime," said Marmalade, awkwardly. "We might be able to do something together then…possibly. And… Hey!" he lunged forward, grabbed hold of Danny's feet under the duvet and yanked his friend down towards the end of the bed.

"Get off!" yelled Danny, who had exceptionally ticklish feet.

Marmalade let go. "I almost forgot. Happy birthday! Here's your card." He dropped a bright green envelope onto Danny's face and grinned. "We'll have a laugh later. Right?"

"Shut up and go away," Ed mumbled from under his bedclothes. "It's Sunday."

"I'm going," said Marmalade in a loud voice while throwing on his clothes. "But you and Ben had better get up. Danny is awake. And it's his BIRTHDAY!"

"Wha...?"

Marmalade hauled off Ben and Ed's duvets and dropped them on the floor, then he headed to the door.

"Where are you going?" Ben yelled after him.

Marmalade looked decidedly shifty. His eyes flicked towards Danny and back to Ben. "I've got stuff to do," he said at last.

Ben frowned. "The sort of stuff we ought to know about?" he said.

"No!" Marmalade hesitated. "No. It's not. I told Danny. It's just stuff I have to do." With that he disappeared out of the door, taking care to close it loudly behind him.

Ben and Ed got up and retrieved their bedding, grumbling noisily.

"He's up to something," Ben muttered to Ed. "I don't trust him when he's like this."

Trick or Treat

They forgot about Marmalade whilst they each gave Danny their cards. He opened the ones from home as well and the three boys sat on Danny's bed, laughing at the jokes and cartoons. Inside Danny's parcel was a pair of Japanese oak drumsticks, a book all about one of his favourite rock drummers and a box of chocolates. The book was one Danny had wanted for ages and he'd dropped loads of hints about it to his mum, but now he had it in his hands he didn't really feel like curling up and reading it. He flicked through and looked at some of the pictures, but they reminded him of his drumming failure, so he put the book down and decided to get up instead.

Ed, Ben and Marmalade had clubbed together to buy Danny a computer game for his birthday. "That should keep you busy for a while," said Ben as Danny unwrapped it.

"Thanks!" The game wasn't about music and didn't have any drumming in it. It was ideal for the way Danny felt at the moment.

On the way over to breakfast Danny's phone rang.

It was his mum, and his little sister. They sang "Happy Birthday", and chatted so enthusiastically about his birthday that he began to feel better about it himself. So maybe he wouldn't be spending the whole day with his friends. But he had a game to play and chocolates to eat. And at least today he wasn't going to fail at his drumming yet again. He was also keeping well away from the corridor to make sure he wouldn't get haunted there again. Things could have been a whole lot worse.

After two chocolate croissants and lots of friends arriving to share breakfast with him and wish him a happy birthday, Danny was feeling okay. What's more, Ed and Ben seemed to have time to devote part of the morning to him.

"We don't need to go and help until a bit later," said Ed. "It's a nice day. Do you fancy a kick around for a bit, or we could try out your game?"

"Great!" said Danny. "Um...what are you two helping with exactly?"

Ben and Ed exchanged glances. "Oh...we offered

to help move some stuff, as we didn't think you'd be about to jam with us today. We thought you'd still be practising. Boring job, but someone's got to do it."

"Here's your card," said Lolly, changing the subject deftly. She handed him the one she and Pop had chosen.

"Have you had anything from home?" asked Chloe, giving him her card, as well as the sweets they'd bought him the day before.

Danny told her about the drumsticks and book, and offered the sweets around.

"He's had loads of cards," said Ben. "Marmalade gave him a really cool one with a great drummer joke in it. It was totally rude, but very funny. And there were chocolates from his sister, but we ate most of those."

"Has anyone *seen* Marmalade?" asked Danny, looking round the dining room. "He went off early, saying he was going to help some senior dancers with something, but I thought he'd be in for breakfast."

His friends looked at each other.

"What?" said Danny. "What's the matter?"

"Nothing!" said Chloe. "I thought he'd be here too." She felt like saying how mean Marmalade was to miss his best friend's birthday breakfast, but she didn't want to upset Danny.

"I suppose it must have gone on for longer than he thought," said Pop. "Whatever he was doing I mean."

"I expect so," said Danny, trying to think the best of Marmalade. "Anyway, it doesn't matter. I'm going to have a kick around with Ed and Ben in a minute. Then, while they go and do whatever it is that they're doing I thought I'd try out the new computer game. Then, in the afternoon…"

"You're going to help with the pumpkin lantern," prompted Chloe.

"Yes. Right. And in the evening…" He hesitated. "I might start my book, or…there might be something good on TV."

It didn't sound a wildly exciting day, but his friends all nodded encouragingly as if they thought it was.

Trick or Treat

"And look!" said Chloe, pointing to the watery sunlight coming through the window as if it was the icing on the cake. "The sun is even going to shine on your special day!"

11 Pumpkin Time

After breakfast, the girls rushed back to their house to sort out their clothes for the party. On the way they met Marmalade, hurrying towards the dining room. He looked rather dishevelled. "Have they finished serving?" he asked anxiously.

"No," said Chloe. "Breakfast is late on a Sunday, remember?"

"Of course!" said Marmalade, looking relieved.

"Where have you been?" said Lolly.

"Can you keep Danny occupied for a while this afternoon?" asked Tara, before he'd had a chance to answer Lolly. "You've got to do your bit to help. We need to decorate the Rock Department, fetch the food and do the pumpkin. We can't risk Danny wandering in while we're decorating."

Marmalade looked worried. "I might not be able to," he said. "I'm rather busy."

"Doing what?" demanded Pop.

"This is your best friend we're talking about," said Tara. "What's more important than that?"

"I've got to go," said Marmalade, ignoring their questions. He set off and then stopped after a few paces. "I will try," he added over his shoulder. "Send him to the main house at about four o'clock. I'll meet him there."

With that he hurried away, leaving the girls looking at each other in bewilderment. "What on earth is he up to?" said Chloe.

"He keeps on disappearing," added Lolly.

"Maybe it's something to do with his tricks." Tara sniffed disapprovingly. "He hasn't managed to get round to all of us yet. But you'd think he'd abandon that to help us with Danny."

"Yes," agreed Pop. "You certainly would."

Back at the house they had fun trying on clothes to complement their witches' hats. Thanks to Tara, they all found something black to wear. Lolly had a fantastic long black dress, but she'd grown out of it. "Here," she said to Tara and Chloe. "One of you should try it on. It seems a pity not to use it."

Tara was happy with the clothes she'd chosen so Chloe squeezed into the dress. "I can't do it up at the back!" she giggled to Lolly, but Pop wasn't going to let that matter.

"Put this purple top on underneath," she said. "Then we can do the dress up with safety pins. No one will notice. And actually, large safety pins could look quite cool."

"Especially if we add more than we actually need," said Lolly. "Turn round, Chloe. Yes," she said, eyeing the back of the dress critically. "We'll make it into part of the design. It'll be perfect."

The time flew by and, all too soon, Chloe had a text from Ed to say that they were leaving Danny playing his game so they could go to the Rock Department to start getting it ready for the party.

"I'll go over and challenge Danny to a game," said Tara. "Someone has to keep an eye on him. I'll bring him to lunch later, and then you can take over while I arrange a time to collect the food from the kitchen."

As soon as they judged that Tara would have Danny safely occupied, the other three girls sneaked over to the Rock Department with the decorations. Ed and Ben already had a heap of masks that they'd borrowed from the props department, and a large bag of balloons Judge Jim had given them. "It's going to take ages to put all this lot up," said Chloe. "And we'll never get all those balloons blown up before lunch."

"But balloons are fun at parties," said Pop. "We'll manage. We can come back and do some more after we've finished the pumpkin."

"Thank goodness we don't have to keep the secret much longer," said Lolly. "But how are we going to stop Danny coming in here this afternoon? That would ruin everything."

"It should be okay. So long as he has a minder

all day," said Pop. "We've done well so far. We can't fail now!"

All was well at lunchtime. Tara and Danny arrived at the dining room, and Danny looked very happy with his day so far.

"I didn't think I was going to be spending much time with any of you," he said. "But Tara came over and let me beat her on the computer."

"That's nice," said Lolly, as if she hadn't been aware of Tara's movements.

"And is it still okay to do the pumpkin with you lot?" he asked the girls. "You know, I've hardly seen anything of Marmalade."

"That's fine," said Chloe, feeling really annoyed with Marmalade. "Eat up! Then we can get started."

Over at the girls' house, Danny was seriously impressed with the size of the pumpkin.

"Wow!" he said, when Chloe brought it into the kitchen. "How are you going to hollow it out?"

"You mean how are *we* going to hollow it out?" she said and they both laughed.

To begin with they all took turns in digging out the golden insides of the pumpkin. They soon had a big heap of it, and Lolly had to find a large bowl to put it in.

"My turn again," said Danny, taking the knife. It was hard work, but good fun, especially with so many of them working together. However, it was taking much longer than Chloe had thought, and she could tell that Tara, Pop and Lolly were getting anxious. They really needed to be back at the Rock Department with the boys to help them finish the decorating.

"It won't be long until we can cut a face in it," said Chloe hopefully. "Bags I do the mouth."

"Remember that one you made when we were at primary school?" said Danny, hacking away, more carefully now he was getting near the skin. "You forgot about making teeth until it was too late."

"And so I chopped up some leftover bits and stuck them in with cocktail sticks!" They looked at each other and laughed.

Pop and Tara had been muttering with each other, and eventually Pop spoke. "We're going to leave you to it, Chloe. You don't need us now." She looked meaningfully at Danny, who was still absorbed with the pumpkin, and Chloe nodded.

"That's okay," she said. "This is the best bit. We're happy to finish it off, aren't we, Danny?" Chloe didn't want to miss the fun of decorating the Rock Department, but she was glad that, for now, Danny seemed happier than he had been for a while.

"See you later," said Lolly. She smiled at Chloe and nodded slightly towards Danny. "You're doing a grand job there." Chloe knew Lolly wasn't referring to the pumpkin, so she winked at her friend and smiled.

"You all deserting us?" said Danny with a grin. "No staying power, that's your problem."

After a bit more cutting and carving, Chloe and Danny stood back to admire their handiwork. "I've got a tea light to go in it," said Chloe. "I'll go and fetch it."

Once the pumpkin was lit they turned off the kitchen light and stood in the doorway, so they could admire the glow. Chloe slipped her hand into Danny's arm and gave it a squeeze. "Happy?"

Danny nodded. "Do you know, I haven't thought about drumming all afternoon! I've been so busy making the lantern I wasn't even tempted to tap out a rhythm with my hands. You were right. I *did* need a break. I feel much better about not managing the piece now."

"That looks lovely!"

It was Mrs. Pinto, on her usual round to check that everything was all right in the house. She smiled at Danny. "Hello, Danny. I believe it's your birthday, isn't it? So, happy birthday! Are you having a good time?"

"Yes," said Danny. "Thank you. It's been fun doing this."

"Are you going to make a pumpkin pie with the bits you've scooped out?" she said, looking at the heap in the bowl.

Chloe looked surprised. "I hadn't thought of that. But we don't have the rest of the ingredients, or a recipe."

"I think I might have," said Mrs. Pinto. "Would you like me to look?"

So a short while later, Danny and Chloe were pushing their pie into the oven, but by the time they were washing their hands afterwards, Chloe was itching to join the others. She worried about leaving Danny, until she remembered Marmalade. He'd told them to send Danny to him in the main house at four o'clock.

"Oh, Danny, I forgot!" she said. "I saw Marmalade earlier. He wanted you to meet him in the main house at four, and it's about that time now!"

"Really? I've been wondering what he's been up to all day," said Danny.

"Me too," said Chloe with feeling.

"See you at tea later on?" said Danny as he put on his jacket.

"Yes," said Chloe. "Thanks for helping!"

As soon as he'd gone she sent a swift text to Marmalade. *It's up to you now*, she wrote. *Danny's on his way.* Then she threw on her coat, and hurtled over to the Rock Department as fast as she could, with the pumpkin lantern.

12 Party Time

The Rock Department was a hive of activity. Ed was holding a stepladder steady while Tara hung the pumpkin fairy lights above the window. Pop seemed to be covering everything in cobwebs and Ben was fitting some orange bulbs into a couple of lamps.

Lolly was setting out the food, and Charlie was sitting on the floor, blowing up the ghost. Several blown-up balloons were drifting about in the draught, waiting to be hung up.

"Where's Danny?" Tara asked Chloe from the top of the steps.

"He's gone to meet Marmalade."

"Good. It's about time Marmalade did something to help."

"What can I do?" said Chloe, going over to Lolly.

"There are paper plates in that box," Lolly told her. "You could put them at the end of the table. And there are the drinks to put out."

"You could help me!" Charlie was looking rather red in the face after half inflating the ghost.

"I don't mind finishing it off," Ed offered with a grin.

"It could do with a bit more, thanks," panted Charlie. "I'm completely out of puff. It's a pity we didn't have a pump."

"Where's the happy birthday banner?" asked Tara.

"Here," said Chloe, finding it on a chair. "If we took an end each we could stick it on the wall opposite the door. Then Danny will see it as soon as he comes in."

"Good thinking," said Tara, climbing down the steps. "Let's do it."

The banner looked really good when the girls stood back to admire their handiwork, but there was no time to waste. It wasn't long until teatime, which was when the party was due to start.

They hung the props department masks on the

walls, where they glowered brilliantly. Then everyone helped out with blowing up the rest of the balloons. The room was soon looking really festive, with the black and orange balloons, lights, the banner and the ghost, that now wobbled in the draught whenever anyone walked past.

"The ghost is really cool," said Pop. "But it does take up quite a lot of space. Why don't we put it at the entrance, to welcome the rest of the year when they arrive?"

"And let's put your pumpkin lantern outside too," suggested Ben. "It'll look great as people come up the path."

Chloe carried her lantern carefully outside and put it on the path. It really did look good, flickering in the dark. And just then Mrs. Pinto arrived with the pumpkin pie!

"I thought you'd like to have it at your party," she said to Chloe.

"That's fabulous!" said Chloe. "Thank you so much."

Soon it was time to put on their Halloween clothes.

Ben's housemaster had given him an old sheet, and he had intended to make a couple of holes for his eyes so he could be a ghost, but he'd kept misjudging the position, and made several holes in the wrong place.

Chloe giggled when he turned away because someone had written *Holey Ghost* on his back. "Did you write that by any chance?" she asked Ed.

Ed nodded. "I couldn't resist it," he laughed.

Pop and Lolly helped Chloe into the long black dress, and congratulated themselves on the success of their safety-pin idea. They added a few more safety pins at the front of the dress, with a little bat and two tiny plastic pumpkins hanging from them, as well as a pumpkin slide for Chloe's hair. They were thrilled with the spooky style they had created.

Soon, other members of the year group began to arrive. Everyone loved the way the Rock Department had been transformed into a cool party venue. Ed started the music, and several people began to dance.

"Any minute now," Ed said. "Marmalade will appear with Danny. Get ready."

Trick or Treat

"There he is!" said Pop, spying Marmalade at the door.

They all got ready to cheer Danny, but Marmalade came in with several senior students, who hadn't even been invited to the party.

"Where's Danny?" asked Chloe.

Tara and Pop looked disapprovingly at the seniors. "What are *they* doing here?" muttered Pop.

The seniors disappeared into the short corridor that led to Judge Jim's room and everyone turned to Marmalade.

"What's going on? Where's Danny?"

Marmalade looked puzzled. "I thought he was with you," he said.

Chloe felt the blood drain away from her face. "But you said to send him over to you at the main house at four o'clock, so I did. I texted you. Didn't you meet him?"

Marmalade groaned. "No! Things weren't going too well and I forgot all about it. My phone was switched off."

"So where is he?" said Lolly. "He can't have vanished into thin air."

But it seemed that he had. No one had seen Danny recently at all.

"We can't have a birthday party without the birthday guest," said Ben, glaring at Marmalade. "You should have been looking after him. We've been working really hard to make Danny feel better and you've done nothing!"

"I…" Marmalade bit his lip.

"Someone will have to go and find him," said Ed. "And as it's your fault he's not here, Marmalade, it had better be you."

"But he could be anywhere!"

"That's your problem."

Marmalade sighed. "I don't think I'm a very good choice," he said. "If I suddenly turn up and try to drag Danny over here he'll think I'm going to play another trick on him."

"That could well be true," said Chloe. "But look, I don't suppose he'll be all that hard to find. We know

he's not going to be practising – and it's teatime. I bet
he got fed up hanging around for you, Marmalade. He'll
be in the dining room, having his tea."

"Genius!" said Ben.

"You go and fetch him!" said Lolly, taking Chloe's
hands. "He trusts you more than anyone. You'll be able
to bring him here."

"Well, all right," said Chloe. "If you think I should."

"We *know* you should," said Pop.

Chloe, wearing her witch's hat and with plastic talons
on her fingers, made her way out of the Rock Department
and down the path. When she looked back, the ghost
was bobbing gently at the door and her lantern flickered
with an orange glow, showing up the uneven teeth she
and Danny had carved that afternoon.

The moon was full and the air was still. The tall trees
nearby cast deep moon shadows and the grass looked
grey, with pearls of moisture glistening on each blade.
It was a beautiful night. She paused to take it all in and

then hurried on. She couldn't wait to see Danny's face once she got him to the Rock Department.

There were plenty of people eating in the dining room and, for a moment, Chloe had problems spotting Danny. Then she caught sight of him at a table by the wall. He seemed very alone in the busy, noisy room, and her heart gave a little jump. She hurried over, so he wouldn't be on his own a moment longer.

"Hi!" He smiled when he saw her, and then his smile deepened. "What *are* you wearing?"

Chloe grinned. "How do I look? Suitable for Halloween?"

"Very cool...for a witch," Danny laughed.

"Hey, I'm sorry about Marmalade not turning up," she said. "I really thought he was going to be there."

"Don't worry," said Danny. "I've had a brilliant time. I want to tell you all about it...but how did you know he hadn't met me?"

"I just saw him," she explained. "In fact...a few of us, including Marmalade are over at the Rock Department waiting for you."

"Oh. Why's that?"

Chloe was already leading the way out of the dining room, and Danny hurried to keep up with her.

"It's difficult to explain," she told him, awkwardly.

Halfway down the steps to the gravel drive Danny suddenly froze. "Oh no you don't," he said. "You're not getting me like that. I'm not *that* stupid."

"What do you mean?" she said.

Danny gave her a triumphant laugh. "You…in your Halloween get up, all ready to give me a good scare on my birthday. Is Marmalade lurking somewhere, with a bucket of water to chuck over me?"

"No!" said Chloe, earnestly. "It's not playing a trick, honestly. I need you to come with me. It's important."

"You'll have to do better than that," laughed Danny, turning to go back indoors. "I'm going to have my tea. I'm hungry."

"Danny?" Chloe felt desperate. Everyone was waiting to greet him and he was walking away. What could she do?

He turned back to her and she held out her hand.

"Please, Danny. We don't have time. You have to trust me. Please."

He began to look a bit uncertain. Chloe took his hand and held it. She looked into his eyes. "You could call it a trick if you want," she admitted. "But it's a treat. It's not scary, or horrible, or even silly. At least I hope you won't think so. It's a good thing, and it's especially for you."

13 Tricks and a Treat

Chloe kept hold of Danny's hand as they walked along the path to the Rock Department together. He was coming, though he still seemed a bit doubtful. On the way, he lifted her hand up and looked at it. "What on earth are you wearing on your fingers?"

Chloe took off her plastic talons. "They were part of my witch's outfit," she said. "But I don't really need them."

She wondered if she ought to take his hand again, to make sure he didn't escape, but to her surprise he took hers instead. So, hand in hand, at last they drew close to the Rock Department.

First of all he caught sight of their pumpkin lantern.

"It looks fantastic," he said. "But why did you bring it over here? And what's that blow-up ghost doing?"

Now, instead of her leading him Danny hurried up the path, pulling Chloe with him. "Is this what you were bringing me to see?"

"Yes," said Chloe. "Sort of."

"Well it's really cool," he told her, pushing the ghost to make it bob about. "But you're not doing much to reassure me. These all look more like Halloween tricks than treats!"

Chloe smiled. "Just wait until you see *this*!" She opened the door and suddenly there was light, and noise and balloons and all his friends waiting.

"SURPRISE!"

"HAPPY BIRTHDAY!"

Everyone yelled as loudly as they could before dissolving into excited giggles and laughter. Danny's friends surrounded him and several clapped him on his back.

He had dropped Chloe's hand in amazement, but now he turned to her with a broad smile on his face.

"I never expected…" he gestured to the happy birthday banner," all this… Why…? And how…?"

"Well, you were so unhappy," she explained. "And we wanted to do something to cheer you up. Then Marmalade thought of a party and it all sort of started happening. We all helped." She gestured towards Ed, Ben, Tara, Lolly and Pop, just in case he thought it was all her doing.

"I'm…gobsmacked," he said. "Wow. I can't believe you'd do all this…for me. It's amazing."

"Come and have some food," she said. "You'd better. It looks as if people have started on it already."

"One thing I don't understand," he said, taking a handful of sandwiches and some crisps, "is what's happened to Marmalade. I still can't see him. But you said he'd be here."

Chloe looked around the crowded room. "Well he *was* here," she said, feeling puzzled, "when I left to fetch you." She didn't want to mention that, apart from having the idea of the party, Marmalade hadn't actually contributed to cheering his friend up at all. "I expect he'll be here in a minute," she said uncertainly. She couldn't help feeling annoyed that Marmalade had even missed Danny's arrival.

But everything else about the party was going brilliantly, and everyone seemed to be having fun. The food was excellent, and people were finishing up the last bits and pieces when someone turned the music down.

"Oi!" said Ben.

Then the lights went down too, until it was almost dark. There were a few squeals from the girls and Danny took Chloe's hand again. "*Now* what have you got lined up for me?" he said with a laugh.

"I don't know," said Chloe. "This has nothing to do with me!"

Slowly, the lights came up a little and, at first, Chloe couldn't see anything different. Then she noticed a grey mist creeping over the floor towards them. The mist swirled and wreathed about their feet in an eerie, billowing caress. Then, over to one side of the room she saw something that made her gasp. It was a strange-looking figure wearing tattered grey clothes. It stood awkwardly.

Danny's hand tightened around hers, until it became quite painful. "The ghost!" he muttered hoarsely.

"No," she said, trying to loosen his grip. "It's pretend. It must be a mannequin."

"Oh." Danny seemed very relieved, but then Lolly let out a terrified shriek.

"It moved!"

As Chloe watched, the mannequin gave a twitch. She grabbed hold of Danny and he put his arms around her.

"What's going on?"

"There's another one!"

"And another!"

To Chloe's horror, the party had been invaded by several of the ghoulish figures. And as they watched in horrified fascination, the mannequins began to move. Stiffly at first, and menacingly, the figures started to make their way into the centre of the room. Some of the girls squealed as they approached, but the mannequins made no sound.

Then Chloe became aware of some spooky music coming quietly from the speakers.

"They're zombies!" she cried.

It was true. Their lurching, shambolic walk, and ghastly appearance proved it. They seemed to be wrapped in tattered clothes, with strips of bandage hanging from what could have been gaping wounds.

The music swelled, to a deep throbbing beat. As they reached the centre of the room the zombies began a hesitant dance, which became more fluid as the music took them over.

Now that everyone was getting over the shock, they really got into the zombies' dance. "They're brilliant!" yelled Danny over the pulsing sound. "They had me spooked back then, but they really are fantastic. Marmalade is amazing, isn't he?"

"Marmalade?"

But Danny hadn't heard her. His eyes were shining with enthusiasm as he clapped and stamped in time to the music.

Trick or Treat

Chloe looked carefully at each zombie in turn. Four of them were quite tall and one was a bit shorter. The more she watched, the more she understood. The zombies must be Marmalade and the senior students he'd brought with him earlier. No wonder he'd hardly managed to help with the party. He must have been spending every spare minute rehearsing!

As soon as the dance came to an end Danny started yelling. "More! More!" Everyone joined in until the zombies had to give in and do their dance all over again.

"I'm sorry I didn't get back to spend time with you this afternoon," the shortest zombie told Danny, when the dance was finally over and they'd taken their bows. "Rehearsals took longer than I thought."

"Don't be sorry," said Danny. "What you did was heroic, especially for you! Getting up early and spending all Sunday rehearsing…for me? I didn't deserve it, but thanks, mate. Thanks a lot."

"That's okay," said Marmalade, grinning through his ghoulish make-up. "I reckon I well and truly tricked everyone before the end of Halloween, didn't I?"

Danny laughed. "You sure did. And I admit I got the message about keeping away from the practice rooms too," he added. "You and your mates really had me scared down in the corridor, thinking the grey ghost was haunting me. Very clever."

Marmalade looked puzzled. "Practice room? No, mate. We rehearsed upstairs in the main house. We didn't go down there at all."

"Are you all right, Danny?" said Chloe. Marmalade had been surrounded by other chattering students and was moving away, but Danny suddenly looked rather shaken.

He gave her a quick smile and shook his head. "It's okay. Don't worry, Chloe. It's nothing. Really. I'm fine."

14 Happy Endings

The music was suddenly turned off again and this time a spotlight pinpointed Danny right in the middle of the room. Pop and Lolly carried in the birthday cake and everyone sang "Happy Birthday". Then Danny spent a while trying to blow out the trick candles and when eventually he managed it, a loud cheer rang out.

"Make a wish!" somebody yelled, and so Danny closed his eyes and thought for a moment, with a grin on his face. But he wasn't out of the limelight yet. Soon everyone was chanting, "Speech! Speech!"

It was clear they wouldn't stop until he'd said something. "Okay," he said with a grin. "Thanks for all this. It was great of you to organize the party and surprise me with it to cheer me up. It's really cool having such a great bunch of friends. But...I must confess I was already feeling a lot happier by the end of this afternoon, so now I feel a bit of a fraud."

"Why? What's changed?" yelled Ed.

"Well," said Danny. "You know how Chloe suggested I ought to take a break from my drumming?" He looked over to her and smiled. "It was all fine until I didn't meet Marmalade this afternoon because he was busy doing something or other else."

Marmalade looked a bit sheepish but everyone else laughed.

"The thing is," Danny went on. "While I was waiting for Marmalade I went into the theatre, and one of the senior drummers was there, putting up his kit for a performance. We got talking and it turns out he knew the piece I couldn't do...and..." he smiled, "we had a go at it together. He gave me a few tips and...I reckon I've cracked it!" His face broke into a wide grin and everyone started to clap.

"Really?" Chloe was looking astonished and thrilled

at the same time. "You didn't say."

"Well," he said. "You turned up in your witch's hat, trying to get me to follow you. Somehow it didn't seem the right time to explain. Sorry."

Nobody else looked sorry. "Play it!" shouted Charlie. "Play it. My kit is in the corner."

"Go on," urged Ed. "Give it a go."

Lolly looked anxious. "What if he gets it wrong?" she whispered to Tara. "Won't he get all miserable again?"

"If he's got it right once he knows he'll be able to do it again," said Tara. "He'll be okay."

"Well I might not perform it perfectly," Danny warned. "Which is why I wasn't going to tell anyone until I'd had another go tomorrow but...okay."

Charlie started to pull his drum kit out from the corner. People moved back to give it space. Ed and Ben helped with the cymbals and Danny positioned the stool. "Watch that hi-hat!" warned Charlie as someone almost knocked it over. "Here," he added to Danny. "You can borrow my sticks."

"Thanks."

Danny slid onto the drum stool and took a deep breath to steady himself. He was still under the spotlight and the room fell silent again. Then he did it. He played the complicated piece of heavy rock he'd been given. He played it all the way through. He did fumble in a few places, but Chloe could tell he was happy with the way it had gone. Everyone gave Danny an enormous cheer.

He got up looking thrilled, and Charlie thumped him on his back. "Gotta hand it to you," he said generously. "You are one awesome drummer."

"I just felt so much looser after the day off," Danny told him modestly. "I was too tensed up before. Somehow, once I didn't care so much, I could do it. You've got to let it flow to play that sort of stuff, and let your limbs take over. I never thought I was going to get it right though. I still can't believe I've done it!"

Suddenly the music was turned up to a full volume, thumping disco beat. "Come and dance," begged Chloe, grabbing Danny by the hand and pulling him onto the dance floor. "I know you don't usually, but please?"

"Okay."

Trick or Treat

Someone grabbed a balloon from the wall, and suddenly balloons were everywhere, floating over the heads of the dancers and being punched from person to person. Marmalade grabbed Pop's hand and Tara and Lolly danced with Ed and Ben. The whole room was jumping.

After a while, the girls were so hot they needed a break. Pop, Lolly and Tara went to open the door so that cool air could flood into the room. They watched as Danny and Chloe danced on.

"I've never seen Danny dance so much," said Pop. "He doesn't usually at all. And they're *still* dancing now!" she went on as the music changed from fast to very slow and smoochy. "Look at them. He kissed her! Isn't that sweet?"

"It's about time," said Tara offhandedly. "I knew they'd get together eventually."

Pop looked scandalized. "You so did not!" she objected.

"None of us did," said Lolly. "But those two... they're made for each other."

Marmalade came and draped his arms over Pop and Lolly's shoulders. "Anyway," he said, still in his costume, and looking decidedly grotesque, "it's a happy ending. And that's the way it ought to be."

✳ So you want
to be a pop star?
✳

Turn the page to read some top tips
on how to make your dreams
✳ come true... ✳

✳ Making it in the music biz ✳

Think you've got tons of talent?
Well, music maestro Judge Jim Henson,
Head of Rock at top talent academy Rockley
Park, has put together his hot tips to help
you become a superstar...

✳ Number One Rule: Be positive!
You've got to believe in yourself.

✳ Be active! Join your school choir
or form your own band.

 Be different! Don't be afraid to stand
out from the crowd.

✳ Be determined! Work hard and stay focused.

✳ Be creative! Try writing your own material –
it will say something unique about you.

 Be patient! Don't give up if things
don't happen overnight.

✳ Be ready to seize opportunities
when they come along.

Be versatile! Don't have a one-track mind – try out new things and gain as many skills as you can.

 Be passionate! Don't be afraid to show some emotion in your performance.

 Be sure to watch, listen and learn all the time.

 Be willing to help others. You'll learn more that way.

Be smart! Don't neglect your schoolwork.

 Be cool and don't get big-headed! Everyone needs friends, so don't leave them behind.

 Always stay true to yourself.

And finally, and most importantly, enjoy what you do!

Go for it! It's all up to you now...

Usborne Quicklinks

For links to exciting websites where you can find out more about becoming a pop star and even practise your singing with online karaoke, go to the Usborne Quicklinks Website at www.usborne-quicklinks.com and enter the keywords fame school.

Internet safety

When using the Internet make sure you follow these safety guidelines:

 Ask an adult's permission before using the Internet.

 Never give out personal information, such as your name, address or telephone number.

 If a website asks you to type in your name or e-mail address, check with an adult first.

 If you receive an e-mail from someone you don't know, do not reply to it.

Cindy Jefferies' varied career has included being a Venetian-mask maker and a video DJ. Cindy decided to write *Fame School* after experiencing the ups and downs of her children, who have all been involved in the music business. Her insight into the lives of wannabe pop stars and her own musical background means that Cindy knows how exciting and demanding the quest for fame and fortune can be.

Cindy lives between town and country – with deer and foxes one side of her garden, and shops and buskers a few minutes' walk away from the other. Her ideas come from both sounds and silence.

To find out more about Cindy Jefferies, visit her website: www.cindyjefferies.co.uk

✸ For more ✸
fabulous fiction, check out
✸ www.fiction.usborne.com ✸
✸
✸